For the real Theodore

Bloomsbury Publishing, London, Oxford, New York, New Delhi and Sydney

First published in Great Britain in October 2017 by Bloomsbury Publishing Plc
50 Bedford Square, London WC1B 3DP

www.bloomsbury.com

BLOOMSBURY is a registered trademark of Bloomsbury Publishing Plc

Text copyright © Katherine Rundell 2017
Illustrations copyright © Emily Sutton 2017

The moral rights of the author and illustrator have been asserted

A CIP catalogue record for this book is available from the British Library

ISBN 978 1 4088 8573 4

All papers used by Bloomsbury Publishing are natural, recyclable products made
from wood grown in well managed forests. The manufacturing processes
conform to the environmental regulations of the country of origin

Printed in China by C&C Offset Printing Co Ltd, Shenzhen, Guangdong

1 3 5 7 9 10 8 6 4 2

One Christmas Wish

Katherine Rundell

Illustrated by
Emily Sutton

BLOOMSBURY
LONDON OXFORD NEW YORK NEW DELHI SYDNEY

It was Christmas Eve, and Theodore was fighting a cardboard box. The box was winning. Someone had been very enthusiastic in their use of packing tape. Someone had thought it was important that the box stayed safe.

The cotton wool was as old as the decorations themselves; it smelt of spices, and old perfume. Most of the decorations were baubles, and most of the baubles had cracked in half. Theo frowned as he took them out. 'You should not be able to cut yourself on Christmas,' he muttered. 'That's not in any of the Christmas carols.'

But at the bottom of the box there were four decorations that were different: a rocking horse, a robin, a tin soldier with a drum, and an angel. The angel's wings were moulting, and the soldier's drum had rusted. The robin had developed a bald patch, and the rocking

horse's rockers had been part-eaten by woodworm.

Theo hung them on the tree, next to the lights
that didn't light. He wasn't tall enough to reach
the high branches, so he tried throwing
the angel at the top of the tree. When
that didn't work, he wedged her in
the branches. He arranged the broken
baubles as best he could.

Theo had found the box of
decorations on top of a cupboard;
his parents had had no time
to buy new decorations.
They had had no time to buy a turkey. Both
of them were at work. An envelope with
gift vouchers inside was the
only present under

the tree. Theo tried to fold the envelope into

a more exciting shape, but it didn't help much.

'You mustn't stay up too late,' his parents

had said. 'We'll be home tonight.'

'But as soon as you can?

You absolutely promise?'

'We promise.' His mother had stroked

his cheek with one hand. Her other

hand was hunting in her bag for

her phone. 'The babysitter will

make you some mince

pies. Won't that be nice?'

Theo pulled a face. *Nobody in the*

world actually likes mince pies, he

thought. But he was a polite

boy, so he only said,

'Why isn't Mrs Goodyere babysitting me?'

'She didn't give a reason,' his father had said. 'She only said she couldn't tonight. And she's getting rather old, anyway. The neighbours say she's becoming a little peculiar.'

'I like her. Actually,' he said, 'I love her.' Sometimes Mrs Goodyere talked to herself, but she gave him chocolate cake with cheese, which was surprisingly delicious, and sang to him at bedtime.

His parents had asked the babysitter to help Theo put up the decorations, but she had fallen asleep at the kitchen table with her nose pressed against her phone.

Theo swallowed. He looked out of the window, because it was less difficult than looking at the tree.

As he looked, he saw a star. It was soaring across the sky, blinking red and green.

'A shooting star,' he whispered. He closed his eyes, and clenched his fists, and crossed his toes, and bit down on his tongue. His father always said, when you wish, you have to wish with your whole heart. Theo thought about his heart, beating hard under his four layers of jumper. (The house was cold, because Theo couldn't reach the button for the heating system.)

He wished with every inch of heart he had. *I want not to be alone*, he thought. He said it out loud. 'I wish for someone to be with. I wish to be un-alone.' He hoped shooting stars did not care about grammar.

He wished so hard his skin prickled and tingled, and his head spun.

Behind him, the tree rustled. Theo whipped round.

The tin soldier was unhooking the loop that held him to the branch, and swinging down the tree.

The angel was trying to fly. Her wings were too threadbare to catch the air, so she sat there, looking half excited and half annoyed, flapping. The robin's wings, on the other hand, worked beautifully, but a twist of wire at his feet was keeping him fixed to the tree. The rocking horse was trying to chew through the string. Its tongue kept getting in the way.

'Excuse me,' said the rocking horse, 'but could you unhook me?'

Theo closed his eyes. The world, he thought, had gone mad. He counted to ten, and opened them. But the world was still there. The decorations were still there. The tin soldier was sitting on his shoe and singing a marching song.

'Your mouth is hanging open, did you know?' The tin soldier was very polite. He offered a tiny tin hand for Theo to shake.

'What … what happened?' said Theo.

'We woke up,' said the angel. 'We're here to keep you company.'

'You – but, I didn't know you could –' said Theo.

'Could you help me down?' said the robin. 'I don't like heights very much.'

'But I – but I – but –' said Theo.

'Excuse me? Boy? Could you unscrew me from my rockers?' the rocking horse asked. 'I'd like to stretch my legs. And rotate my ankles. I've been dreaming of it.'

There was a screwdriver in the kitchen. Theo made sure not to wake the babysitter. The unscrewing took some time, because the rocking horse tried to eat Theo's hair, and although he apologised, he couldn't quite make himself stop.

'That feels *astonishing*,' he said. He cantered up and down the mantelpiece, and jumped over the photo frames. He only broke a very few.

Theo's eyes were aching from staring. 'What happens now?' he said.

'Anything you want to happen,' said the angel. 'I think we woke to do whatever it is you need. We've woken up before, and that's always what we've done

in the past.' She paused. 'It doesn't always go that well, actually.'

'So – I can choose what we do? Anything at all?'

'Anything at all.'

Theo shut his eyes and thought. His eyes were closed for quite a long time. A cough came from his shoulder.

'I don't want to interrupt your thinking,' said the rocking horse, 'but, just while you're doing it – I wonder if you might have something to eat? I'm hungry.'

Theo didn't know what rocking horses ate.

He had a feeling real horses ate sugar lumps, and carrots, and apples. He ran to the kitchen to get them. The apples were soft and wrinkled, and the sugar didn't come in lumps, but the carrots were crisp and fresh. He chewed on one himself as he ran back to the tree.

By the time he got there, it had turned out that rocking horses also ate pine needles, electrical cables, and the bottoms of curtains. It ate the apples – even the one that had started to look like somebody's great-grandmother –

with a great deal of chomping and burping and sighing with happiness.

The rocking horse had barely swallowed the last crumb of electrical cable when a voice came from Theo's elbow.

'Excuse me, boy. You wouldn't be able to do me a tiny favour, would you?'

It was the robin. He had a businesslike beak, and polished black eyes. If he could have worn a tie, Theo thought, he would have. But as he spoke, the red on his breast blushed a deeper scarlet.

'I seem to have forgotten how to sing. I know I knew once: I remember it very vividly. I had great talent. But I can't remember how. And I'm a robin.' The robin's voice cracked. 'All real robins sing. Can you teach me?'

'Oh – I'm so sorry!' said Theo. 'But I don't know how you explain singing. It's just something that happens. Like dancing. Or farting.'

'But there *must* be people who can,' said the robin. He sounded angry, but Theo could see that he wasn't. He was excited, and anxious, and hungry, which often come out sounding cross, but are in fact more complicated. 'You can teach *anything.*'

'There's a woman called Mrs Goodyere who teaches the piano, just down the road,' said Theo. 'But she wouldn't come tonight. And it's late.'

'Could we go and visit her?' said the robin.

'I'm not really allowed to leave the house alone.'

'Says who?'

'My parents.'

'But they're not here, are they?'

'No,' said Theo. He looked very hard at his shoes. 'No. They're not.'

'And you wouldn't be alone,' coaxed the robin. 'You'd be with us.'

The walk took longer than it usually would have done, because the rocking horse kept stopping to eat leaves, and twigs, and snow, and bits of other people's cars. He had to be discouraged from eating the dog poo.

Mrs Goodyere was awake. She sat at her piano, but she wasn't playing it. She had a picture in her hands.

They rang the doorbell. Mrs Goodyere answered, still holding the photograph. She did not seem at all surprised to see a wooden horse nibbling her doormat.

'Theodore!' she smiled down at him. 'I'm sorry I couldn't babysit – I thought I'd like to be in my own home tonight. I've been remembering my Arthur. What was it you wanted?'

Theo explained the problem, while the robin tried to look unembarrassed and bold. In fact, he looked like he was trying to swallow an unusually large insect, but facial expressions are difficult for robins.

Mrs Goodyere shook her head. 'I'm sorry, my dear. I have no qualifications in teaching birds.'

The robin fluttered his wings anxiously. 'Would you reconsider for a fee? I cannot offer payment, but

I believe robins are skilled at catching worms. Do you enjoy worms?'

'I'm afraid I'm more of a tea and cake person myself.'

'Or – if you were wanting to do some remembering, perhaps I could remember with you.'

Mrs Goodyere looked harder at the robin. 'You know – you actually look rather like my Arthur,' she said. She hesitated, with the door half open and half closed.

'I would be honoured to hear about him,' said the robin. 'He sounds very handsome.'

'Well – I could try to teach you a scale,' said Mrs Goodyere. 'I've never taught a bird, but perhaps children and birds aren't so very different.'

They all came in. The angel tried on a teacup as a hat.

Mrs Goodyere sat down at the piano. 'Listen. Sing this note.'

The robin let out a noise somewhere between a squeak, a wail, and a cough.

'That's a good beginning,' said the old woman. 'Again.'

Each time, the note got clearer.

Theo kept an eye on the other decorations while the robin sang 'Away in a Manger'. It wasn't easy. The rocking horse had to be discouraged from eating the piano. The tin soldier caught sight of its reflection and tried to attack it, just to pass the time. The angel tried to fly again, and crashed into the china cupboard.

'Sorry,' said Theo to Mrs Goodyere. 'Sorry!'

'Why don't you take your friends home, dear, and I'll send robin back when he's worked out the high notes? And perhaps he and I will have a little bit of chocolate cake, and talk about the old days.'

'It would be a delight,' said the robin. He gave the closest thing that a robin can give to a bow. 'I am at your service.'

They paused outside the house, while the horse ate the hedge.

'What's that?' asked the angel. 'A spare wing! A wing, just lying there!'

'It's a feather,' said Theo.

'Does it belong to anybody?'

'It would have belonged to a pigeon, I think.'

'Could I borrow it?'

'I don't think the pigeon needs it back,' said Theo. 'I think you could have it for good.'

The angel's eyes widened. 'Are there *more*?'

'More pigeon feathers? I think so! I mean – there's definitely more pigeons. So it would be logic that there'd be more feathers.'

The angel bit Theo's hand to make sure he was paying attention. 'Where? Where would there be more?'

'There's a wood, down by the library. We could go feather-hunting.'

The rocking horse was untangled from the hedge, and they set off. The angel kept the rocking horse's head warm. Theo held the tin soldier in his gloves.

The night was clear, and the stars shone as if they knew something important was happening down below.

'There are often feathers under a bird's nest,' said Theo. 'We'll find a nest.'

The bird's nest they found had been abandoned when the birds had flown south, and was half full of snow. Theo unplaited the feathers from the nest.

'I'm afraid they're quite little,' he said.

'But they're beautiful,' said the angel. 'They look so warm.'

hey searched amongst the trees for an hour. Theo's gloves got soaked with snow, but the horse licked his fingers to warm them up. Eventually they had a pile as high as the angel's knees: blackbird feathers and pigeon feathers and a few that were pure white.

'Look! Oh, this is wonderful! How do I fix them on to my wings?' asked the angel.

'With glue, I think,' said Theo.

'Glue! How glorious! Do you have any glue?'

'Oh. Well, no,' said Theo. 'Sorry.'

'At home?'

'No,' said Theo.

'We can buy some!' said the horse. 'I remember about buying things from last time we woke up. I distinctly remember enjoying it.'

'Does anybody have any money?' asked Theo.

'Christmas decorations don't really have money. Or handbags,' said the tin soldier. 'Or legs, usually.'

'Oh,' said the angel. 'Well. Oh.' She tried hard to smile. 'Thank you. For trying.'

Theo put his hands in his pockets, and tried not to show how much his heart suddenly hurt.

'Wait, look!' He drew out a packet of chewing gum, and began to chew hard. The angel chewed even harder, her jaws working furiously.

The tin soldier was still too rusty to be much help, but he tried. The rocking horse ate his first two sticks of gum, and Theo refused to give him any more.

They made tiny balls with the chewing gum, and stuck a ball to the bottom of each feather.

The wings grew. They were a bit sticky, and they smelt a little pink, but they were beautiful.

The angel was shaking with nerves as she flapped her wings.

'What if they fall off?' she said. 'What if I fall down?'

But the feathers stayed on. She rose. She wobbled. She pulled her hair back behind her ears. And then she *soared*. Up, over the trees, over the chimney pots. Theo sat on the horse with the tin soldier and watched; they clapped and cheered even when she was much too high in the sky to hear. Theo gave his best whistle, using two fingers. The tin soldier banged his drum.

She looped the loop around a lamp post, and built a snow angel on top of the church spire. Then she spun around their heads, and disappeared into the stars. 'Lots of things to do!' she called to them.

heo and the tin soldier and the rocking horse sat staring up at the sky. It began to snow.

'Theo?' said the tin soldier.

'Yes?' said Theo. He felt sure the tin soldier was going to ask for something. *A hat, perhaps*, he thought: *one of those tall furry ones that soldiers wore outside palaces.* He'd quite like one himself.

'I'd like,' said the tin soldier, 'to be able to play my drum. It's so rusty: listen.'

He tried to bang his drum, but all that came out was the crunching, scraping noise of rust on rust.

'We can definitely try,' said Theo.

They didn't have any oil, but they discovered that snow and rocking-horse spit and

the corner of
Theo's sleeve polished
the worst of the rust off the drum.
Theo used a pine needle to gently
scratch the rust from the soldier's ears.

At last the tin soldier gave a great *rat-a-tat-tat* on
the drum, and a cat on the pavement opposite looked
disapproving and ran up a tree.

'It's loud,' said Theo approvingly.

The tin soldier smiled, but his smile was not as
wide as Theo's. He bit his tin lip. 'The thing is: I think
I need someone who I can play my drum *for*. I'd like
someone to be in love with.'

'Oh!' Theo was startled. 'That might be rather difficult. I don't know many tin people I can introduce you to. Are you sure you wouldn't rather have a furry hat?'

'Yes!'

Theo thought hard. 'Would she have to be tin?'

'No! She'd just have to be kind.'

'I have an idea, then.'

hey rode the rocking horse to the biggest toyshop in town. The horse picked the lock with his tongue.

At the door, the tin soldier hesitated. 'Do you think I should I smarten myself up first? I have a feeling you're supposed to brush your hair if you're hoping to fall in love.'

'But you don't have hair.' Theo was envious. He hated washing his hair.

'But it's the principle of the thing,' said the tin soldier.

Theo found a pen in his pocket, and drew back the soldier's hair so it shone dark and glossy in the lights of the security camera. They went in.

They passed rows of dolls: dolls with ringlets, dolls that really cried – 'Much too young,' said the tin soldier – dolls with high-heeled shoes and dolls with no feet at all that lived inside each other. And then –

'That's her!' cried the tin soldier. He jumped up and down, and the sound of his tin feet on the floor echoed through the shop.

Theo lifted down her box. She wore a princess's gown, and her eyes were closed, as if she were wishing.

'That's her! That's her!' The tin soldier's voice clanked with emotion.

'But how do you know?' Theo looked up at the doll, worried. 'You can't love someone just because you like their dress, or their hair, or their face. Everyone knows that.'

'It's not that! It's not that at all! She *waved*.'

The princess's eyes opened. She smiled a smile so large it ruffled the hair around her ears.

'Hello,' she said to the tin soldier. 'I like your drum.'

She bunched her skirt up around her knees and climbed out of the box. Then she hesitated, suddenly shy.

The tin soldier blushed a bright tin-can red.

Theo nudged him
forward with one finger.
'I can play it for you, if you like,'
said the tin soldier.

44

'I'd like that,' said the princess. 'Yes please.'

The tin soldier played Theo's favourite carol. He was a little rusty, but the sound rang loud and sweet through the toyshop. It sounded of new beginnings, and of fresh years.

A dinosaur tried to applaud. Its arms weren't in fact long enough, but everybody appreciated the effort.

'Can you dance?' asked the princess.

'I'm not sure,' said the tin soldier. 'My joints are still a little stiff. But I can try.'

The soldier and the princess danced down the aisle of the toyshop while the rocking horse sang, out of tune, a song about love.

Theo left a note at the cash desk in his best handwriting.

They made the rocking horse spit out the teddy bear he was eating, and slipped out into the night.

'Theo? There's one other thing,' said the tin soldier. He held his princess tightly by the earlobe. (They were still learning how to be in love.)

'Is it a furry hat?'

'No! It's just – I'm a soldier, aren't I?'

'Well. Yes. You're a drummer,' said Theo.

'But I have nobody to fight. I need a war. And I have no weapon. I need a gun.'

Theo looked at the tin soldier. His voice was gruff, but his eyes were very kind. Of course it was hard to tell, with tin.

'Soldiers don't need wars,' said Theo.

'Yes, they do!' said the soldier. The princess nodded hard in agreement.

'No they don't,' said Theo. He was certain. 'Soldiers protect things. People, and cities, and homes. Come with me. I have an idea.'

They rode through the town towards the centre. The streets were empty, and the snow came up past the rocking horse's ankles. Theo gripped the reins tightly. The princess and the soldier swung from the ends of the rocking horse's mane.

They stopped in the town square.

'There,' said Theo. 'There's something that needs protecting. It's a baby.'

'A *wooden* baby?'

'Well, yes,' said Theo. 'But I don't make fun of you for being made of tin.'

He set the soldier and the princess down next to the ox and the ass and the wooden manger. He gave the princess a large stick. The rocking horse chewed it to a sharp point, just in case.

The princess gave a few experimental jabs, and stuck the stick up Theo's nostril.

'It works,' she said. 'Good.'

The two of them took up their positions, one each side of the wooden baby. The soldier's tin hat glinted in the starlight. The princess used the train of her skirt to cover the baby's feet.

'You can leave us here,' they said. 'We'll stand guard.'

It was very late by the time Theo and the horse arrived back at his front door. The snow had begun to fall more heavily, and Theo had lost all the feeling in his toes.

The rocking horse waited for Theo to tumble off his back. He licked Theo's nose and hands. He licked the inside of his ears. He chewed one final piece of Theo's hair.

Then, without a word, he turned and galloped away, away from the lights of the city, out into the wide spaces of the world and the snow.

The house was dark. The babysitter was still asleep. Theo curled up under the tree – there was just the tinsel, now, and the broken baubles, and the lights that didn't light.

It's just me, now. I'm alone, thought Theo. *It's just me, all over again.* He gave a tiny shiver, and tucked his knees up under his jumper. He fell asleep.

The next thing Theo knew he was being lifted in a pair of arms. He twisted to look, but found he was too tired to open his eyes. But the arms around him were strong, and the jacket smelt very familiar.

He heard his father's voice above his head. 'He's asleep. It's odd – his shoes are soaking wet.'

Theo closed his eyes tighter, and gave a little snore.

He wriggled, trying to arrange his face and neck to look like someone who has been playing quietly, inside, all evening.

'We must get him less itchy pyjamas.'

It was his mother's voice. 'It's very good to have you home, darling. I thought you'd be hours yet.'

Theo swayed in his father's arms as he was carried upstairs. His father gave a low laugh. 'I know it's absurd, but I thought I saw a horse galloping past my office without a rider.'

'A horse? Are you sure?' said Theo's mother.

'It was probably just a shadow. Or a bicycle. But I suddenly wanted to be at home so much I could hardly breathe,' said Theo's father. 'So I dropped everything and ran for the next train.'

Theo's mother's voice was full of wonder. 'But I saw exactly the same thing! A horse cantering past my window. And I longed to be with you and Theo so wildly that I left without finishing the sentence I was typing.'

'Do you remember,' said Theo's father, 'when we bought those Christmas decorations? It was our first Christmas together. It reminded me of that day.'

'Me too, me too! Could we have been dreaming?'

'Perhaps. Although it was eating a windscreen wiper as it ran, which is odd, in a dream horse.'

Theo's mother laughed. 'Come on,' she said. 'We've got work to do.'

Theo peeked out through his eyelashes, and saw them tiptoe from the room, their arms around each other's waists.

heo ran downstairs on Christmas morning so fast he missed half the steps and landed with his big toe in his ear. He scrambled up.

From the sitting room he heard the sound of something that was very nearly music. It sounded like a robin trying to sing 'Away in a Manger', and struggling with the high notes.

Theo dashed into the room. A robin sat outside in the rising sun. It was perched on a snow-covered branch and it was singing and singing and singing for joy.

The whole room blazed with light in gold and silver and red, casting light on the pile of presents. The tree was hung with so many baubles it jangled like a peal of bells when Theo breathed on it. The tinsel that lined the pictures was as thick as Theo's arm.

A Christmas pudding and a freshly baked chocolate log sat in the middle of the table, steaming gently.

Theo's parents stood behind him in the doorway.

'Where did it all come from?' gasped Theo.

'I don't know,' said his father. His eyebrows were dancing.

'It wasn't us,' said his mother. Her mouth was very serious, but her eyes were not. 'I think it must have been the magic.'

Theo ran to the window. There was a mark on the glass, as if someone – or something – had licked away the frost in a message of pure, giddy love. The same someone had eaten part of the letterbox.

Theo ran to look at the parcels. One of them felt soft under the wrapping paper; it seemed to be the shape of a tall furry hat.

Theo's mother knelt beside him under the tree. His father brought in three mugs of cocoa; Theo's was heaped so high with cream that when he took a sip it got into his eyebrows.

Then he looked up, and saw an angel sitting at the top of the tree. Her wings were white and black and grey, and they shone with frost. From certain angles, she seemed to be winking.

It turned out, much later, that it hadn't been a shooting star at all. There are no red and green shooting stars. It was an aeroplane, flying towards Belgium. But even aeroplanes heading towards Belgium can work magic, if you have luck and love and Christmas on your side.